KT-434-402

Did you see them too?

Neil Griffiths

Illustrated by Janette Louden

I thought I saw
an elephant,
sitting on
the stair.

BRISTOL CITY LIBRARIES
WITHDRAWN AND OFFERED FOR SALE

Bristol Library Service

AN 3133082 7

Red Robin Books is an imprint of Corner To Learn Limited

Published by
Corner To Learn Limited
Willow Cottage • 26 Purton Stoke
Swindon • Wiltshire SN5 4JF • UK
www.redrobinbooks.com

ISBN 978-1-905434-05-3

Text © Neil Griffiths 2007
Illustrations © Janette Louden 2007
First hardback edition published in the UK 2007
This paperback edition published in the UK 2008

The right of Neil Griffiths to be identified as the
author of this work has been asserted by him in accordance
with the Copyright, Designs and Patents Act 1988.

All rights reserved.
No part of this publication may be reproduced, stored in a
retrieval system, or transmitted in any form or by any means,
electronic, mechanical, photocopying, recording, or otherwise,
without the prior written permission of the Publisher. Any person
who does any unauthorised act in relation to this publication may
be liable to criminal prosecution and civil claims for damages.

Design by
David Rose

Printed by
Tien Wah Press Pte. Ltd., Singapore

For Jill, a dear friend
who has brought lots of
laughter into my life.

Neil x

BRISTOL CITY LIBRARIES

AN3133082 7	
PE	26-Mar-08
JF	£5.99

But when I looked again, it simply wasn't there.

Then I saw a python, hanging from the light.

But when I looked again, it had vanished out of sight.

And next
I saw a bear,
hugging
my TV.

But when I looked again, there was nothing I could see.

I even saw a monkey,
swinging on the door.

But when I looked again, it wasn't there anymore.

But when I looked again,
it had disappeared
from view.

Then I saw a lion, yawning on my bed.

But when I looked again, it was my teddy bear instead.

And yes I saw a penguin, washing in the sink.

But it had gone too, in the time it took to blink.

Are they really there,
or could it just be me?

I'm getting rather nervous
at what I might
next see!